MULBERRY DOON

MULBERRY DOON

Stories and Poems

Michael R. Milano

Full Court Press
Englewood Cliffs, New Jersey

First Edition

Copyright © 2014 by Michael R. Milano

Published in the United States of America
by Full Court Press, 601 Palisade Avenue
Englewood Cliffs, NJ 07632
www.fullcourtpressnj.com

ISBN 978-1-938812-30-9
Library of Congress Control No. 2014932756

Cover Art by Miriam Katin

Editing, Book Design, and Author Photograph
by Barry Sheinkopf for Bookshapers (www.bookshapers.com)

Colophon by Liz Sedlack

DEDICATION

To my wife, Patricia,
and all the other wonderful women
who have graced my life.

Acknowledgments

As before, this book has had many readers and commentators to refine my writing. Pat is my most important critic and inspiration, but here are a few who left significant contributions: Bob Ghiradella, Paul Murphy, Sarah Franz, Monica Hodges, Annette Hollander, Barbara Lederer, and my poetry reading group—Bob, Pat, Jon, Jeff and Addie. Betty Carpenter did the heavy lifting of preparation and was the scribe for "Longhand," and Barry Sheinkopf, as before, edited exquisitely.

The cover for *Mulberry Doon* is the work of Miriam Katin, a friend and talented artist with several published graphic novels. Remarkably, she is also a lifelong devotee and depicter of the mulberry. It is she, sitting in the mulberry tree, who is the child appearing in the story. How often does that happen?

TABLE OF CONTENTS

Introduction

*M*ULBERRY DOON, *like its predecessor,* Conversations and Poetry, *balances prose pieces and poems. After a reading in Leonia, I confessed to Fred Stern, the arranger of the reading, that I had finished writing poetry books. One was enough. He said, "No, you'll write more. I know." To my own surprise, I kept generating poems and then short essays. Thanks Fred, for the challenge. This is the last one, and I mean it.*

Mulberry Doon begins with four stories. The first two are rather literal elaborations of dreams. "The Solution" was an incredibly long and complex dream that touched on many of my pet topics, including Thomas Malthus, overpopulation, and the fatal power of unrecognized guilt. The science is approximate, so don't give up peanut butter. Only the dialogue was added to the dream itself.

"Transference" is, to me, deeply personal and meaningful, a manifestation of hard-won insight. In my analysis, a constant complaint was my inability to generate the "right" kinds of dreams for me and for my analyst. The memory lingers, and "Transference" tells the story in contemporary form.

"Choke Artist" is, well, true. It's a feeble attempt at making lemonade from ancient lemons. The childhood memories are dressed in contemporary form. History comes around twice: first as tragedy and later as humor. Who said that?

"Mulberry Doon," the title story, arose from a stray thought while riding along the Bronx River Parkway. What would my life have been like if I had been a mulberry? I got the giggles but the absurdity seems to make it work. I hope it has some of the charm of Miriam's cover.

STORIES

THE SOLUTION

"The constant effort towards population, which is found even in the most vicious societies, increases the number of people before the means of subsistence are increased."

"The superior power of population cannot be checked without producing misery or vice."

—*Thomas Malthus (1766–1834), British social economist*

I HAVE ALWAYS CONSIDERED MYSELF a conventional American citizen, if not a model one. My work has focused around thirty years of teaching and doing neurobiological research at Rutgers University, and around twenty years as science editor of *The Record* newspaper of Bergen County, New Jersey. I am a devoted family man, the father of two lovely girls, and an aging relic of the peace movement. Like most scientists, I am well educated but in other ways unexceptional. I like being unexceptional. Imagine my surprise at the following phone call: "Hello, this is Charles Ryan, assistant to Marjorie Glover, Secretary, Homeland Security. We have come upon a problem of great scientific importance and are asking your assistance. We must act quickly. Secretary Glover would like to meet with you in Washington, D.C. tomorrow at 1:00 PM."

". . .Can you tell me what the questions is? My specialty is neurochemistry, and I don't see the connection with government," I said.

"Unfortunately, I cannot divulge details before the meeting, but we need your assistance."

I don't know any terrorists, nor do I have membership in any radical groups. I smelled a rat. What could Homeland Security possibly want with me? Did they know of my participation in antiwar protests following September 11, the catastrophe that spawned Cabinet status for Homeland Security? I am idealistic, but middle age has made me cautious. What could be the science? My instinctive response was, *Stay out of this, it smacks of danger.*

However, my curiosity, and a vague craving for excitement, began to wage a tug of war with my caution. "Yes," I said, "I'll be ready."

"Fine," said Mr. Ryan. "I will arrange automobile transportation, plane fare, lodging, and meals. We will pick you up at 4:00 PM. We are deeply grateful for your participation."

He got the wheels rolling, and I spent the night at the Mayflower Hotel, a venerable Washington institution and the prior business location of the Mayflower Madam, Sidney Biddle Barrows. I learned that Uncle Sam doesn't underwrite sex or extravagant dining. Fear had trumped hunger, though, and my meager allowance was sufficient for whatever appetite I had left. I had gone there hesitantly, without knowing the purpose of my mission and with limited trust in my government. I slept alone in a disappointingly simple room, and I slept poorly.

The Department of Homeland Security (DHS) occupies thirty-five acres of nondescript office buildings in D.C. It looks strictly government issue. Even this attempt to minimize attention unsettled me. "Still, it's not the NSA," I told myself.

After a pat-down, weapons check, and a few bureaucratic interactions, I was ushered into Secretary Glover's office. There were the customary American and Departmental flags and inscribed photographs. Paintings of former Secretaries Michael Chertoff, Tom Ridge, and Janet Napolitano looked sternly at me. The office was elegant, but nothing about the proceedings thus far reassured me. Secretary Glover was attractive, but she, too, had already mastered the portrait stare. This was serious business, and I was in the dark.

"Secretary Glover, this is Doctor Michael Bruno, the researcher from Rutgers University," said Ryan, and he left.

"Doctor" sounded good. I needed reassurance. My medical credentials might help to create the sense of authority I needed, which everybody else seemed to have.

Secretary Glover began, "Thank you for being here. We have a matter of the utmost importance to discuss. It's of the highest delicacy and confidentiality is essential. The President has set a high priority on this project. The President asked me to look into the activities of Dr. Davis, the reason for asking you here. The President is hosting the World Peace Conference in two months, and discreet resolution of our problem on an urgent schedule is needed."

It seemed impertinent to interrupt at this point to ask, "What is it all about?" So far, Glover had the reins and was impervious to any note of anxiety from me. I guess highly focused people are that way.

"We sought you out for multiple reasons. You are an experienced neurochemist and have written papers on the interaction of nerve cells and viruses."

"True, but—"

"As a journalist you can be counted upon to keep quiet and protect your sources. We have already done a quick background check and know you have a top-secret clearance from prior Army work. This project will be conducted on an eyes-only basis, and your report will go only to me." She leaned forward and added, "I cannot impress upon you the importance of this project and of its confidentiality. No one is to hear of this, including your family. We are asking you to do a great service for our country."

I was stricken with a rising sense of unease. "Will there, uh, be any danger to myself or my family?"

"No, there won't—if you honor our contract for confidentiality."

"Can you please tell me the nature and duration of this assignment?"

"Well, the Department recently employed an eminent neuro-biologist, Dr. David Davis, for research on aggression and potential use in war. Initially, it was a joint project with the Department of Defense. Dr. Davis was given permission to use laboratory animals in order to explore which neurological pathways facilitated aggressive behavior. We were hoping to find novel interventions for wartime purposes. Pending approval by the Human Research Board, Dr. Davis would then later be allowed to study humans, of course with their signed consent and with no foreseeable harm. We were hoping for a new weapon to disable aggression. After completing his authorized studies, though, Dr. Davis abandoned his agreed-upon protocol and conducted toxic experiments on humans. To date, a hundred and eight unknowing subjects have died. His covert actions have placed us in a perilous political position. The Department of Defense has turned the matter over to Homeland Security. Can you imagine the ramifications if this becomes public?"

"Of course, of course," I said.

"Furthermore," she continued, "Dr. Davis has refused to divulge the methodology and scientific basis for his work. He worked alone and without corroborating scientists. He is a proud and stubborn man who is difficult to decipher, and he has not been forthcoming about his behavior. He is a loner and has no family we can interview. We have exhausted our methods of interrogation and need someone with your background and skills to debrief us about his research. The public has been protected from knowledge of this project, and we intend to keep it that way. After interviewing Dr. Davis at length, you will prepare a confidential report to be sent only to me. I would estimate a week's time for your assignment. Can we count on you?"

"Yes, I understand," I replied, but what in hell did I understand? Genocide? A government cover-up? Enforced secrecy? What were the dangers to me? Secretary Glover had offered scant assurances.

As I was considering my apprehensions, she plunged onward, with me in the wake. "A car will pick you up at 8:00 AM and take you two hundred miles to the federal penitentiary in Lewisburg, Pennsylvania, where Dr. Davis is being held. There is nothing more I can say now except to express my deepest concern about the project and profound gratitude for your participation. We will talk again when I receive your report." She still seemed unconcerned and unaware of my trepidation. I was on my own in uncharted territory, awash with anxieties.

My next stop was Lewisburg Federal Penitentiary. Its French Renaissance facade, replete with Gothic arches and corbels, was quaint. The gracefulness stopped there. Al Capone, Alger Hiss, Jimmy Hoffa, and John Gotti had all done time in that maximum-security building. Dr. Davis had joined a royal lineage of criminals.

That afternoon, after more pat-down and another weapons check, I was ushered into an apple-green interview room with two uncomfortable chairs and a simple desk. More government issue.

There was no evident recording device. It was straight out of *Law and Order*. Before me, in prison orange, sat a slender, balding, bespectacled fifty-year-old with a clenched mouth and a puzzled, anxious look. *This is a genocidal maniac?* I thought. I had been expecting Hannibal Lector; instead, the fellow resembled Mister Peepers. I was feeling at least as disconnected from reality as I could imagine. Remembering lessons from my own psychoanalysis and from years of teaching, I decided first to establish a personal connection. Friendship was too much to aim for, but we needed a bridge of scientific fellowship to create the possibility of a revealing interview. I may have needed it more than he, for I anticipated a severe struggle. Dr. Davis' reputation was forbidding. So was Homeland Security. I was in the middle. Thus far, everything I had gone through bore a tinge of malevolence and danger.

"I'm Michael Bruno," I said, extending a hand, trying to effect a casualness I hardly felt. I skipped the doctor part, hoping to establish a conciliatory mood.

"Doctor David Davis," he said coolly, ignoring my proffered handshake, his mood suspicious and severe. He had pink skin and the pale blue eyes of a Vermont churchgoer, set in an oval face. His cheeks were very slightly drawn, his thin lips inexpressive. "Have a seat."

I took one. It scraped against the concrete floor when I moved it. "I—uh, I've been aware of your ground-breaking work at Rockefeller Institute, on the interactions of viruses and neurotransmitters, for a long time. I've incorporated some of your contributions into my own research, and I've found your ideas to be quite original and stimulating." I was hoping our mutual scientific backgrounds might minimize my role as interrogator, but anxiety was trumping artifice, and my words were stiff and unnatural.

I nevertheless pressed on. "I'm here as a scientist at the invitation of Homeland Security. I need to discuss the nature of your research on the neurobiology of aggression. The rationale, and your methods, are of interest, but the results of your intervention are of greatest importance. As you know, your final experiments were unauthorized, and they have apparently created a major stir at Homeland Security. To date, they tell me, a hundred and eight people have died. So far I know nothing substantial about your project, and I hope our interview will be both amicable and searching."

"Yes, the results," he said. He leaned backwards, tense and inscrutable. "I had reached one of the most significant advances in modern science, the capstone of my career. This was science at the highest level and of potentially great importance to man's survival on this planet. Now Homeland Security has destroyed all evidence of my research. I have nothing to show for it but my memories. Secretary Glover is dishonest, deceitful, craven, and a political animal uncomprehending of science. I am sick to death and helpless against a herd of bureaucrats intent only on silencing me and protecting themselves."

A dead silence hung in the air as I contemplated this. "Can we continue?" I asked. "I am truly sorry about your present predicament," I added, though nothing had yet stimulated sympathy for the righteous Dr. Davis.

"If you can be honest with me," Davis said, "we can continue. One lie, and we are finished. I've had enough of that from Homeland Security, and I've had enough for today."

Such were his terms. I agreed, though that night, alone in my Lewisburg motel, was agonizing. How could this detached, unemotional man of science commit genocide? He was forbidding, distant, and unfriendly, but he had already succeeded in controlling our interview. He should have been the one on the defensive. The immediate question was, who was most tense: Homeland Security, he, or I?

The answers emerged as he plunged into the interview the next day. He had on a fresh prison uniform, though he was wearing the same government-issue laceless sneakers. "Since the topics I was asked to study were aggression and population control," he began, "the first thing you should know is that, for twenty years, I have been a member of the Malthus Society. We believe that the world can support only one and a half billion people indefinitely. Today we have four and a half billion workers, vying for only one and a half billion sustainable jobs. The present population of six and a half billion, rocketing toward ten, will deplete the earth of irreplaceable resources and lead to incredible famine and war. At the present birthrate, this will be inevitable. According to Malthus, the future will be catastrophic. I don't see how these observations can be challenged."

How could I doubt these facts, these conclusions? Because they were uncomfortable? A new level of unease was rapidly growing in me. Dr. Davis was going global, but the implications were unclear to me. What could his intention possibly be?

"The Society discussed possible solutions to rampant overpopulation and felt that convincing five billion people to surrender their reproductive rights and not pass on their precious DNA would be doomed. People are addicted to the idea of some form of eternal existence. They want children, and more children, and damn the consequences. Political solutions—passing laws, I mean—would be impossible. No politician would touch a proposal that controversial. Their only concern is reelection, not the future of man. Improvements in agriculture and technology, the present strategy, will inevitably be overwhelmed by the continuing growth of population. Global warming is already almost unstoppable.

"People are stupid, though, when they're confronted by such terrible realities. They always wait too long to acknowledge the problem and accept the need for change. . . . Rather than meekly accepting calamity, I, a scientist, undertook the search for a solution. Got it?"

So far he had not recognized my presence or feared its significance, nor did he seem in any way affected by doubt about the effects of his experiments. He was truly operating only within his own world.

"I already had research approval from the Departments of Defense and Homeland Security, to work with animals to find the neurological pathway through which aggression is expressed, which could possibly lead to elimination of combatants. My theory was that aggression was so intense in some animals that, deprived of it, they would die rather than live in peace. If the same findings applied to humans, this could be used in war—or, in my secret ambition, for reducing the population burden of the Earth. I decided that, if I were to radically cull the human population, I should start with the worst people, criminals.

He shifted on his metal chair and cleared his throat before his hands reassembled themselves in his lap. "I was given a laboratory at NIH. As background to our intervention on bad people, I needed to do research on animals, specifically animals with strong patterns of aggressive behavior. Their demise had to be peaceful and quiet, without awareness, protest, or suffering. . . . It was a daunting challenge. Monkeys, like humans, can be impressively bad. They, I mean the monkeys, would have been too expensive for my research, however. Rabbits and dogs are too docile. Rats, however, share ninety-eight percent of their DNA with humans. They're cheap, and everyone hates them. So we settled on rat subjects. At that point, the government saw it as an aid to the war effort. How much more could I expect them to comprehend," he added, a faint smile fluttering across those thin lips, "and why would I tell them anything?"

By then my curiosity was soaring. Where was he heading? Rats? Humans? The implications of his Malthusian theory were terrifying, and contemplating a solution even more repugnant. I felt a forbidding sense of secrecy, but where was the science in his plans?

He proceeded. "First I chose the meanest, nastiest Norwegian rats and inbred them for six generations until I had truly evil creatures. They bit and killed one another and horribly bullied the weak. They were, in short, the ideal non-human vehicles for the study of badness and aggression. Since evil, like everything else, has a pathway in the brain, I had to first isolate the part of the brain where badness originated, and then define how it spread to the cerebral cortex, where action is decided upon and initiated. If I could then find a way to cripple that pathway of badness, the rats would lose their aggression, fall asleep, and die. Such, I hypothesized, would be the beginning of the solution I was seeking."

What he saw as the solution was rapidly becoming a major problem for me. As a moral being, I could hardly listen. As a scientist, I had to. It was already too late to back out.

"I gave radioisotope-labeled glucose to the rats during their worst behavior," Dr. Davis continued. "Positive Emission Tomography—you know how PET scans work, I assume—then identified the anatomical areas of greatest metabolic activity by outlining the regions of increased concentration of the glucose during aggression.

"I was excited when the enhanced metabolic activity pointed toward connections between the amygdala, the seat of emotion, and the frontal cortex, the part of the brain associated with planning. This subdivision of the median fore-brain bundle was selectively hyperactive during evil acts, suggesting that we had isolated the primary neurological pathway of aggression and badness in the rat's brain. I had identified the point of origin, but finding the effective roadway of badness was just the start. I then had to locate the neurotransmitter serving as the chemical driving force of the pathway. This was the Achilles heel of the rats—and perhaps humans. If there was a pathway for badness, there had to be a pathway for other human traits. Expanding the research would be easy considering what I had already accomplished. We could target greed, perversion, and, if necessary, traits considered to be altruistic. There would be no limit to the flexibility of my techniques," he concluded on a note of self-satisfaction.

That night I called home. As I talked with my adolescent daughters, I began to absorb the impact of what Dr. Davis was unfolding. His research was his child. My children were real, and full of life and dreams about the future. They, and I, harbored hopes about coming generations. Would we be among the saved or the doomed? I imagined Dr. Davis sleeping. I did not.

The following day, he continued reporting on his research. "Next I placed nanotubules in the involved areas and isolated a gamma amino butryic acid derivative, 4-6 amino 8 hydroxyl GABA, which was present only in the affected area of the brain initiating aggression and was most active when the rats were at their worst."

He was on a roll and consumed by these achievements. He still seemed unconcerned about my reactions. "This molecule was the fuel for the 'bundle of badness,' as I called it. It was to be the target for destroying the GABAnergic pathway of aggression. To confirm my hypothesis, I administered the hydroxyl GABA directly through the tiny tubules, and the rats immediately displayed intense aggressive behavior. The behavior requires the neurotransmitter, but the GABA alone can stimulate the behavior without environmental provocations. "Once the pathway was disabled, the rats, deprived of their badness, would tire, sleep, and peacefully expire. So I hoped. Since humans are also notably aggressive, I hypothesized that they would be vulnerable to the same intervention. I needed only a means for selectively attacking the 4-6 amino 8 hydroxy GABA. By then, Homeland Security had begun to show increasing interest in my ongoing research. This was annoying and intrusive, but, since I was making progress, I continued the search for ways to disable the pathway. I was reassured by their scientific ignorance.

"Of course, I would eventually need access to bad *humans*. I convinced Homeland to provide a lab right here in Lewisburg Penitentiary, which has turned out of course to be profoundly ironic. There are lots of bad people here, and they could be bribed with favors or reduced sentences to participate in what they were told would be harmless tests. At first we would interrupt the neural pathways and transmitters, but I had still only partially completed my studies on rats.

"Happily, the GABA derivative was found to be involved only with aggression and badness. Neither serotonin, nor norepineph-rinergic and other neurotransmitters, played a role. Undoubtedly this quirk was an evolutionary relic, but it was a fortunate one. I could now focus my attack on a single molecule. Simplicity is a key to success. But I needed to find a potentially lethal agent that would bind itself silently to our target neurotransmitter. Barclay's, a herpes simplex variant, was perfect. It could be secretly dissem-inated by air and was undetectable by ordinary means. The virus, following its affinity, would selectively and imperceptibly attach it-self only to the 4-6 amino 8 hydroxy GABA, rendering it a target for destruction. When we found a way to activate the virus, it would destroy the GABA and the pathway dependent upon it. Whichever bad rat—or humans—had been exposed to the acti-vated virus would fall asleep and die. I was one step closer, but at that point the rats had yet to show any ill effects."

As the outline of Davis' project grew clearer, my sense of re-vulsion increased. The goal of exterminating the bad rats and, in later stages, bad people, was horrifying. Extending "The Solution" for eighty percent of mankind was unthinkable. After the bad ones, who else would go? Who would live? Who would decide? Who would comfort the bereaved? There would be so many dead and so few survivors, who could bear to go on? *How could he not be aware of this?*

"I had accomplished this in only six months," Davis continued, "but I lacked the means of activating the virus already bound to the rats' neurotransmitter. The next step involved experimentation with numerous chemical activators. 'Fortune.' said Pasteur, as I'm sure you know, 'favors the prepared.' One day, quite by accident, I was having lunch in the laboratory and unwrapped a peanut butter- and-jelly sandwich. As the fumes from the sandwich suffused the laboratory, the experimental rats began to die. Apparently the peanut butter-and-jelly aroma had activated the Barclay's virus. The bad rats, behaving as predicted, then fell asleep peacefully and died. By targeting as yet unidentified pathways and neurotransmitters for additional emotional states, this type of intervention could be the future vehicle for later removing people with and without badness. The solution to Malthus's quandary was in my hands."

I shifted in my seat. "...Dr. Davis, I am impressed by the originality of your scientific research, but so far you've described only rats being killed." Recalling my introduction by Homeland Security, though, I could see the direction of his ideas. I was awed by the isolated, unfeeling nature of the man, which allowed such guiltless plans. Five billion dead? Progress? Scientific triumph? Personal achievement?

"Just when success seemed around the corner," an agitated Dr. Davis continued, "Homeland Security, damn them, stepped up their visits. I believe they were frightened to be associated with such an important but controversial discovery. I admit, applied to humans, it did raise a few concerns. But I strongly advocated that this might be the only solution to worldwide overpopulation and pestilence. While it was drastic, in time mankind would revere my contribution to saving the planet."

At that moment I had been convinced that his coldness was not just a veneer. A complete absence of feeling was his *only* state.

Then a cloud of rage crossed his face, followed by a smile of triumph. At last feelings had begun to show, but they too were abhorrent. "Homeland Security announced plans to shut down my lab, and swore me to *secrecy*. The *cowards*! I was desperate. I had not even begun to study humans. It might take years to get approval for humans, and even then consent would be doubtful if death was the result. My research might end up applying only to rats. So, ignoring protocol, I released a small amount of Barclay's virus and peanut butter-and-jelly vapor into the prison and the neighboring community. I. . .naturally I wore a protective mask, for my own safety, even though, unlike the prisoners, I didn't have an active pathway of badness as a target. I was aiming at a sample of both bad and unselected people, hoping the bad ones would behave like the bad rats.

"The results were evident in two days. Thirty percent of the inmates died. So did thirty percent of the guards. These findings were exhilarating. My hypothesis was confirmed. However the following question remained: Why had the guards died?"

I was appalled. This was both hideous and the height of inhumanity. Would Dr. Davis have received a Nobel Prize or a Hitler Award for his work? With his next statement, the answer became clear. "In the environment outside the prison, thirty percent of the general population also died. A whole convent of nuns went to sleep and died. Eventually a large number of young children were found dead in their sleep. I had not anticipated these results, but I felt they were especially promising, since the effect of suppressing population growth would extend to future generations. These children would never have children, and I would have the template for eliminating the five billion surplus people killing the earth. I was still puzzled by the effect on non-specific, non-aggressive, clearly not "bad" people. But since more people died, the experiment was a total success.

"Then, in my moment of triumph, Homeland Security got word of the results and immediately destroyed my laboratory, bad rats and all, and buried my chemicals. They created a fiction that the cause of the hundred and eight deaths was an unexplained virus that had already spent itself as a local plague. They locked me up and threw away the key. I am silenced forever, and my discovery lost to mankind. I have made the most significant scientific advance in modern times, and it will never be implemented. . . . I doubt that you can make any difference," he added, those pale eyes suddenly fixing mine with a wild concentration, "but at least someone else knows."

At this he did show another flicker of emotion—not regret over his actions but frustration at not being allowed to terminate eighty percent of all living humans. After the bad died came the good, and then the innocent. He seemed incapable of noticing the difference. He was enraged at Homeland Security.

I was enraged with him. Our interview had occurred within the confines of the infected prison, and the duration of lethality was unknown. Had I been infected? Was I vulnerable, like the thirty percent, or safe like Dr. Davis, who saw no evil in his work? What would Glover do with this information? The public outcry would be overwhelming.

The immorality of the plan was monumental. I had been granted access to the scientific basis for genocide, disguised as the salvation of humanity.

But as a fellow researcher, another question remained. All scientific questions must be addressed. In science, the quest for answers is sacrosanct.

What was the meaning of the pattern of deaths? What was the vulnerability that affected prisoners, guards, ordinary people, nuns, and little children? I slept poorly for the next two nights, trying to comprehend what I had seen, heard, and felt. I reread Freud's *Criminals from a Sense of Guilt;* volumes on sociopathy; Hannah Arendt; and of course, *Why Bad Things Happen to Good People.* I was possessed by the search for a scientific answer to the odd pattern of deaths.

The weekend was a chamber of horrors. I would call home and later, alone, weep in my motel room. But I also saw the logic and the devastating importance of Malthus's and Davis's ideas. Oh, I was aware that Western intellectuals eat thirty-dollar lamb chops while the sub-Saharans starve. Of course, we should help with aid. But what if they, and we, were going to starve anyway because we are humans and we proliferate, dominate, and destroy everything? Dr. Davis had had the courage to see this and the ingenuity and monumental lack of empathy needed to devise a solution. Thanks to him, I was now a knowing participant instead of an ignorant by-stander. But if he was inhumane, I had no better answer to the problem. So I pondered.

Eventually the explanation of Dr. Davis' mysterious results became clear to me. The answer was *guilt*, people's way of *feeling* bad about themselves for unconscious reasons *without* harmful wrong-doing. It opened the pathway of self-loathing through feelings of badness and overt aggression, irrespective of significant actual deeds. In fact, guilt is always disproportionate to evil actions. Churches are full of people who feel guilty, and prisons are full of people, about seventy percent it seemed, who are unburdened by such sensibilities. Actually *being* bad or aggressive was not *necessary*. Such feelings were just as effective, and Dr. Davis's science and logic had failed to account for this. The bad who acknowledged their actions died, but so did those with inner feelings of guilt who were, in fact, innocent of significant wrongdoing. They only felt an immature need to be good. I was prepared now for our next meeting.

"Dr. Davis," I began, "there has been a fundamental mistake in your research. You isolated the pathway for being aggressive and evil in rats, and found an ingenious method of using a neural pathway to kill them. People are different. In humans, the pathway for being or doing bad is the same pathway as that for *feeling* you are a bad person. Feelings of guilt are the explanation for human vulnerability in your experiment. Only thirty percent of inmates feel they are bad—the same -for guards and the general population. In fact, people who try to be better are often the most guilt-ridden ones. They are not good enough. So they *see* themselves as bad. All nuns feel they are bad. That's why they're in the convent. Little children, with immature superegos, feel they are bad for not eating their peas or for biting their brother. Good, bad, and innocent alike die! Such is the impact of unforeseen guilt on your experiment."

He seemed puzzled, and another flicker of emotion crossed his face. I could see it as a tightening of the flesh around his eyes. Was it curiosity or something deeper, perhaps guilt? Would he continue to be cold and defensive in the face of this information?

"Well," he said, "I hadn't thought of that. You are saying feelings can be as powerful as acts? I admit I hadn't considered that. . .but my research may still be the only solution to Malthus's predicament. At any rate, the scientific values of my discoveries are unquestionable. The dead subjects who committed no bad deeds are collateral damage and cannot negate the importance of my findings."

He ended on a note of defiance, but I knew there were more acts to come in the play. What could happen in the man's unconscious?

As I returned to Lewisburg the following Monday morning, I was feeling elated. Malthus remained unanswered, but I had scored a coup. I had come to an understanding of the mystery of the pattern of deaths resulting from Davis' experiment. This was a matter of scientific significance that had received scant attention from the man himself. But then, feelings were simply of no consequence to him, nor were the deaths of innocents.

I entered the prison bristling with curiosity and the desire to file the final pieces for my report. I could not imagine what Dr. Davis would say about my analysis. Would he insist only on the value of his work and not see the tragedy? Would he—could he—have heard and felt? Could he have seen his blindness, his imperviousness? Was there a seed of regret beneath his lack of empathy and for his failure to see the consequence of his experiment accurately?

I met the guard who routinely scanned me before my interviews with Dr. Davis. My mood was immediately deflated by his facial expression. I knew him to be a kind person, kind even to the difficult Dr. Davis. "I'm sorry to have to tell you this," he said, "but Dr. Davis died peacefully in his sleep last night. . . . You know, he really liked you. You and I were about the only people he talked to. Our medical staff has not yet identified the cause of his death. Oddly, his last communication was an urgent request for a peanut butter-and-jelly sandwich."

First comes lightning, then comes thunder. I was reeling from this information. I alone knew the cause. I had killed that man, the final paradox. My information had implanted guilt and left him hopeless and helpless. He had killed a hundred and eight, but I had killed him. His suicide shook my world to the deepest degree.

Since then, my course of action has been inescapable. To hell with DHS and my enforced vow of secrecy! Let the bastards deal with their own mess, and let Marjorie Glover do to me what she wants. I will reveal Dr. Davis to the world. I will write an account of this tragedy and send it to the *Washington Post* tomorrow. Dr. Davis must be recognized and studied for his brilliance, his accomplishments, and his fateful rational cruelty. Blindness and inhumanity, even in the service of science, kill. So too does a governmental cover- up. Too late, even Dr. Davis came to see this, but his work, good and bad, will see the light of day.

Malthus's problem remains un-addressed. It is ironic that the insight I gave to him also destroyed him, but I had had no choice but to confront him with the meaning of what he had inadvertently done. The bad feel good, and the good feel bad; guilt confounds, and the best die. Dr. Davis's scientific coldness, detachment, and lack of feeling had kept him from seeing this. Only those with an ability to look into the soul can penetrate some scientific problems. I only hope that something besides that man's death will come from this tragic error. In the meantime, I have been writing feverishly, and am feeling very tired and must take a long nap. My work is over except for adding the final details of this experience. Sleep beckons.

TRANSFERENCE

(for Richard Yazmajian)

TRANSFERENCE IS A PSYCHOANALYTIC TERM *that, in its narrowest form, describes feelings about persons and situations from childhood that are projected onto the neutral presence of the psychoanalyst. In that setting , dreams and feeling states can be "analyzed," and the underlying conflicts resolved. "Transference," the short story, is another iteration of the effect of my father's death on me as seen through the light of transference toward the analyst. The writing is introduced by two previously published poems, "I Became a Doctor" and "Loss". The poems provide the background for the actual dream rendered almost literally in the story The next expression of loss is the transference, wrapped around the dream as presented in an analytic session. There are three expressions of the theme of loss. The first is the poems. The second is the dream itself, and the third is the struggle to elicit a response from the analyst to reassure the dreamer about abandonment. A fourth example of resolved transference might be the dedication of the story to the elusive analyst who forced the dreamer to come to grips with his own feelings. The dream ends in resolution.*

I BECAME A DOCTOR

As my eleventh year was ending,
I stood silent in my bedroom, watching,
shaken by the nightlong struggle
of my father in the vestibule of death.
While the doctor worked to save his life,
I looked on from one to five AM.
This is what I saw:

purple lips and mottled skin,
rasping sounds of labored breathing,
fluid bubbling from his mouth,
semi-conscious, eyes rolled back,
bruises where the doctor drew huge vials of blood
to bring his pressure down.

Though he lived three years beyond that crisis,
not yet twelve, I knew
Our time together would be brief.
Through that night I chewed the hated cud of helplessness.
Neither could I swallow it, nor could I spit it out.
At dawn I slept, a child, awakening a doctor.
Then I learned new words describing that which I had seen:

cyanosis,

dyspnea,

pulmonary edema,

phlebotomy,

purpura.

Strange that merely different names
bring me comfort, but they do.
Words are simply kinder than the pictures.

LOSS

I've borne a loss for fifty years,
in a silent hidden space
with room for only me
and for my long-dead shadow.
The burden comes in many subtle ways,
but mostly in the stubborn, dogged
need for goodness, camouflaged as work.
So gripped, I stumble through my days
of numbing toil, the secret sore inside.

He didn't choose it, nor did I.
If he had seen, could he have spoken words

that I, at fourteen, could have grasped?
And who could see the soul transformed,
laced with guilt and obligation?

The hardest part is debt unpaid,
the ledger closed too soon
and I forever in the red.

ENTERING MY ANALYST'S OFFICE, I gave my usual furtive glance, hoping to see something of the man I heard from so rarely. I always could feel his presence and felt it was a caring one, but how would I really know? I've never feared ghosts, but this one felt powerful in an incomprehensible manner. Often I lay on the couch wrapped in the involuntary obsessive practice of counting the holes in the ceiling tiles. Resistance. My dreams and associations were repetitive and disappointing to me. How, I thought, could he stand it week after week, if I barely could? However, today would be different. Today I had a prize offering.

"My dream last night," I began, "was deeply felt. I have no idea what triggered it, and it was somewhat frightening."

No response came. I was aching for a word from him, some reassurance of his presence. Still I knew nothing would be forthcoming, so I donned my cloak of obedience, repressed my anxiety, and went on.

"My father and I were going out for dinner. I don't know who made these dinner plans, my father or me. I've often felt uncertain about our closeness or lack thereof, so my levels of hope and anxiety were always bumping up against one another. But here we were, he at the wheel and I the navigator. We hadn't talked in years. What would we have to say? More to the point, what would I have to say? I think Freud said, 'The most important day in a man's life is that when his father dies.' That's not the problem here," I said to my analyst, but perhaps it was. In my dream I wondered, What would tonight's encounter bring? Would this be a reunion and rebirth?

"My choice for dinner was a Cuban restaurant in the Bronx. Something exotic. It was like me to choose something out of the way and strange to my father. It also spoke of my need to impress him and even intimidate him a bit. Our loss of familiarity over the years, and the heavy burden of expectations, created a distinct sense of unease for me. I hardly knew who he was or what to expect from him.

"My troubles began as we drove to our destination, a restaurant off Broadway onto Clinton Street. The location might have been a reprise of a harrowing search for a restaurant, WD 50, on Clinton Street in Manhattan. I'd had only vague directions, and I'd been distracted by the noisy and chaotic street life—pedestrians everywhere. I could barely read the street signs as they flew by. Each time I pleaded to slow down, my father laughed dismissively and sped up. This flustered me further and heightened my sense of humiliation until, magically, I saw signs for Clinton Street. We turned left and immediately came to our nameless restaurant. My confidence was already damaged.

"He left me off at the restaurant and drove off to park the car. I went inside, confirmed our reservation, and looked over the menu. Black bean soup, *lechon asado*, *ropa vieja*, and *flan* were familiar and enticing. My spirits rose and I began to focus on the evening to come. I warmed up a bit and stepped back outside into the cool evening air, rapidly turning cold, to await my father's arrival.

"Fifteen minutes later, I interrupted my vigil and stepped back inside to warm myself. I remember now that I hadn't seen his face in the dream—it was more an intense awareness of his presence. In fact, I had never seen his face in any dream. But in the dream I was warm again, and I exited to wait and greet him. Minute by minute my composure eroded. Where had he gone? He couldn't have forgotten me, or had he? After forty minutes alone and with no call from him to the restaurant, I panicked and began to walk the neighborhood, searching for him, the car, or a parking garage. As night fell, I wandered through a warren of Bronx streets with no idea where I was. I also had no wallet, no money, and no orientation. My sense of hope was dwindling.

"Everywhere I searched, I passed clubs and restaurants with expansive glass fronts. At first they were unobtrusive and sparsely populated. As night deepened, they were illuminated by a golden glow. Music drifted through them. Partners whirled in the sensuous movements of salsa dancers. Everywhere there was excitement, love, celebration. I, however, was on the wrong side of the glass."

Still no comment from my analyst.

"The restaurants grew gayer and brighter while I grew more and more desolate. I was cold and had no car, no wallet, no cash, and now no father. Gradually my feelings about my predicament became infused with anger. *Where did he go? Why did he leave me in such a condition? Was it a ruse?* I had hoped for a renewal, a connection. How could he have done this? Every ten steps my anger escalated a degree, but I was still alone.

"As the restaurants and clubs closed and the streets emptied, I began a frantic search for money to call home and reestablish the love, comfort, and security I had known. At an all-night deli, a stranger offered to secure cash if I would access an ATM with him. When we got to the machine I asked his name. But when I turned around, he had vanished. Even petty crooks had abandoned me. There was no help anywhere.

"So I did what down-and-out people everywhere do. I walked the cold and empty streets: perplexed, anxious, and angry. Every stranger I met I asked, 'Which way is the George Washington Bridge? Which way is New Jersey?' I harvested a bushel of strange, blank looks. Throughout that long night solace, direction, and care were nowhere to be found, either within myself or in the outer world around me. I was alone. Where had he gone?

"At last, daybreak oriented me to east and west. I headed directly south, with the sun on my left. Soon I saw Yankee Stadium. How had I traveled so far south? No matter. With the sun at my back, I crossed the 155th Street Bridge into Manhattan. I walked cross town to Broadway, where I headed north to access the George Washington Bridge. I knew now that I would arrive home soon. My night of fear, anger, and disappointment would be over."

At this point so was the dream. Recounting it had been so intense that I had been unaware that my fifty minutes had elapsed. Usually, I counted each minute, hoping for both more and for less at the same time. I had even lost track of my sense of my analyst's presence. He had not spoken. No surprise. Now I had to choke back my curiosity about the dream and about him and reenter reality. Another lonely task.

"That is an important dream. We will talk more about it tomorrow," he said.

I returned to work.

THE CHOKE ARTIST

1. A player who succeeds in playing so fantastically bad that it is considered a form of art.

2.Someone who is incapable of competing effectively when the situation calls for it.

3.A player who makes a career of faltering in the clutch situation.

——The Urban Dictionary, online, 2013

I T'S UNUSUAL TO COME OUT of the closet this late in life, but it has become even more onerous to hide in shame from something I have recognized since childhood. At first I tried to deny it. Then I sought change. I took lessons, practiced, prayed, and even got psychoanalyzed. Nothing helped. Still I bore the stain. I was, am, and always will be a choke artist. There. The cat is out of the bag.

Very few people have bared their soul about a flaw so deeply rooted in shame and hiding. For me, it started in childhood. Doesn't everything? I still recall freezing at an eighth-grade piano performance, my one and only public recital. Of course, I had hosted weeks of anticipatory dread. I finished the piece (*Für Elise?*) and soon thereafter quit piano lessons, a frequent course of action for choke artists. There are other examples too mundane or private to report. And no, it's not about sex. That would have been really tragic. Sports, the commonest form of choking, were impossible to give up. I was just too invested.

As a child I had lots of time to daydream, a dangerous habit. Books and school came easily. I even belatedly learned to play with other children. Perhaps my fantasies were just too intense and I had no siblings to kick me around and disabuse me of my sense of importance. I was, to quote my mother, "Your typical hothouse flower."

My head teemed with baseball statistics gleaned from reading *The Sporting News* every week. There were heroes (Yogi Berra, Jackie Robinson) and cads (Ted Williams, Enos Slaughter). My godfather, Ray Kinnon, a Boston bookie, took me to Red Sox or Boston Braves games every day for two weeks over four or five summers. We sat in the right-field bleachers, where he encountered numerous "friends" laying bets on the horse and dog races. At home, I listened to Red Barber call Brooklyn Dodger games and dreamed of Ebbets Field. Each night at 6:00 PM, Marty Glickman did a replay of the last Dodger, Giant, or Yankee game. His only prop was two pencils to click together to mimic the sound of the bat on ball.

When television appeared, Sunday afternoon in the fall belonged to professional football: the New York Giants and the other founding NFL teams, the Lions, Browns, Redskins, etc. Lou "The Toe" Groza kicked field goals with a missing right big toe. Bingo Bingaman, "The Immovable Man," weighed over three hundred pounds. In those sweet, innocent, pre-steroid times, that made him a physical phenomenon. Whitehall, my hometown of 3,500 or so railroaders, had a respectable semi-pro football team, the Pachyderms. They seemed like giants to me. I loved them and loved the name, which for many years was the longest word I knew.

Friday belonged to *Gillette Fight Night* and Saturday brought the roller derby, two displays of utter mayhem and violence. Golf and tennis, and even skiing, were for big-city dudes. Ice skating ruled in Whitehall. I had ample experience, but to my disappointment, I never learned the hockey stop or skating backwards. They were cool, but I couldn't quite commit myself to the act. Furthermore, my ankles were, and are, like boiled lasagna noodles.

Hunting and fishing were major activities in Whitehall. They were totally choke-free, since there was no crowd when you were reeling in a perch. If you shot a squirrel or rabbit, no one clapped. It was a nice feeling, but mostly it was dinner. I'm sure that if I, as a deer hunter, ever had a ten-point buck in my scope, I would have fired and missed. Even the deer would have booed.

You can see where this is going.

Like hundreds of millions of other American boys, I hungered to be a good athlete. Not a great one, just an adequate one. I was at least sane enough not to crave greatness, even on a small scale. Whitehall High School, with fifty-five students in each of its four classes and half of them farmers who were busy in the afternoons, offered ample opportunity to the mediocre. I was slow and short, but fiercely determined. Lots of fantasies and limited gifts: another hint of what was to come.

BASKETBALL

was my least favorite of the three major sports. My father had nailed a rim to a rickety garage over a cement square. Even though the rim was only eight and a half feet high, I couldn't come close to dunking. Did I say that I was vertically challenged? At that time, dunking was an undeveloped art anyway. Friends would come around and play horse. At night at the rec field we played pickup basketball. I played one entire game with a broken foot.

Despite a surplus of desire, I was never better than a below-average player. But, as advertised, Whitehall High School needed warm bodies for every sport. So I became the twelfth man on a ten-man basketball team. I got to showcase myself in practice: I played tenacious defense, took adequate care of the ball, and had a lousy shot.

I played J.V. as a sophomore, and varsity after spending most of the time on the bench rehearsing what might happen during my rare appearances in games. We lost most games. Worse, game in and game out, I never scored. Not once in two years. The pressure

rose, and I began to wonder if any of the Whitehall spectators no-
ticed. I just wanted to get the gorilla off my back. Finally, in one
of our last games, I was alone, cutting to the basket on a fast break.
This was our basic practice and game time warm-up drill. It was
familiar and it was easy. My moment had come.

I still remember, in slow motion, everything about that shot.
The ball felt very heavy and seemed to cling to my hand as it left.
"Oh, God, please let this go in," I muttered to myself. Most of all
I remember the clang as the ball bounced off the rim to the floor.
I had thrown a brick and was doomed to remain forever scoreless.
Then, as every choke artist knows, I felt the presence of the crowd.
It was a Whitehall-sized crowd, and they gave a sympathetic but
audible groan. The crowd knew, the cheerleaders knew, my team-
mates knew, and, worst of all, I forever knew. No one on the bench
or anywhere else ever said anything. Welcome to becoming one of
the insiders concerning my infamous basketball choke.

FOOTBALL

was another sad story. I weighed a hundred and fifty pounds, hardly
dominating. As a slow outside linebacker, I ate a lot of dust. But I
was, God knows, committed. The coach queried me about my fail-
ure to step it up in games. Ten-percent better performance was
expected as a matter of course. How could I tell him that, in prac-
tice, I gave a hundred percent every day, every play? There was
nothing extra in the tank. I was decent at the brute skills of block-

ing and tackling. And I was comfortable as long as I stayed away from the ball. But, then, it's tough to choke without the ball. Unfortunately, every sport revolved around a ball.

My senior year, the coach was searching for a backup quarterback for practice and in case of catastrophe. Given the limited options, he considered my academic potential first. I was a quick read. So he swallowed hard, handed me the play book, and said, "Learn it." That was easy; I did it overnight. The next day, I ran a few simple plays in practice. I never ever threw a pass. That would have been far above my pay grade. I was beginning to recognize that academic brains and sports brains came in different containers.

My moment of truth came toward the end of my final year in a game against Granville High School. I was put in during the fourth quarter for mop-up duty. The game already had been decided. Still I was nervous. My first play was a pitch-out to the running back going right. I wheeled and pitched the ball into a large vacant area to the left, the wrong side of the field. As the ball left my hand, I knew that I had blown it and disgraced myself. It was the classic flashback of desperation for the choke artist. Too late.

I took to pressure like an elephant takes to ballet. I was not exactly your go-to guy, and it was another moment of ignominy. Fortunately, it was an away game, and most of the Whitehall fans had left, so I shrank in solitude. Did we win two games that year? Who remembers?

BASEBALL

was my deepest love and my last bastion of hope. I listened to the Brooklyn Dodgers on the radio and went to major league games in Boston. This was Gerber's baby food for my dreams. My father schooled me by hitting grounders on the gravel that was another part of the backyard. The chicken coop backed me up. I got adept at handling bad hops, which were a plague at every level of Whitehall baseball.

Our backyard abutted railroad tracks. Sliding under two fences and crossing the tracks, I would reach an open sandlot field where, throughout childhood summers, I played baseball from breakfast to dinner. I was a reasonable sandlot hitter and, on one glorious occasion, we completed a triple play.

My baseball playmates were three of the eight Valastros, who lived across the tracks next to the sandlot. Later I learned that my grandfather had given them the house after their father died. I was not so generous. I unintentionally became their scourge. Patty Valastros was a pretty, athletic girl two years my senior. I hit a line drive (softball) that broke her nose. *Ouch!* Carmel was a catcher. I took a big swing, and the bat came around and hit him squarely in the temple. After a few anxious moments, Carmel regained consciousness and the game resumed. Oops. Concussion? It was still the twentieth century, remember. Chronic traumatic encephalopathy had not yet been invented. Freddie, whom I remember as the oldest Valastro, played third base ahead of me on the varsity high school team. In a scrimmage, he charged the plate in an obvious bunt situation. I pulled the bat back and smoked a line drive into Freddie's cup. He folded like a shut clam. Against the Valastros, even the butcher boy play worked. If only I could have played every game against them.

When I reached the varsity, it was good field, no hit. I wasn't afraid of the ball hitting me; I was praying that it would. Even a walk would do, since I knew I wasn't going to hit the ball. My lack of confidence seeped through my pores. The more the pressure, the worse I felt. In addition, I had a truly feeble swing. I ended up batting ninth: not good for the fantasy life.

My ultimate debacle came on a sunny day in May. By the seventh inning, we were still in the game. I was playing second base and ran to short right field to take a relay and throw out a runner at the plate. As I wheeled to throw, the damnable voice spoke: *Be careful to throw it straight to the plate.* Fatal advice. As the ball left my hand, I knew that I had choked again. Once again, that rawhide seemed glued to my hand. It floated to home plate in a high, long, lazy, sleepy arc, reaching its target two or three steps after the runner had scored. I cringed. I should have winged it, even if it landed in the third-base dugout.

That would have been an error instead of a choke. If nothing else, it would have been briefer and less craven.

No one on the bench commented, but I spent several games on the pines. Fortunately, no fans—not even one, not even parents—went to any home *or* away baseball games. The team my senior year was an 0-for (no wins for the season), so everyone tried their best to forget the whole experience. And now that I think of our record, it occurs to me that there may have been eight other choke artists on the field with me.

GOLF

was a new opportunity. After three major sports, I'd had three major-league chokes. I can't even remember the little ones. But golf offers great advantages to the choke artist. There were no spectators, no teammates to disappoint, no ball-in-the-hand thing, and nothing in the *Whitehall Times*. True, the golf course regularly humiliated me, but it humbled everyone else, too. I learned to curse softly at myself and play on, relatively unperturbed.

Then I began playing golf with my brother-in-law, Terry, an excellent athlete. We started to play for small bets, five-dollar Nassau. Then I really wanted to win, at least occasionally. I developed a pattern of breaking out ahead and folding in the stretch, a form of protracted choking. The climax to the chapter was truly brutal.

One day, when I was hitting the ball reasonably well, we came to the eighteenth hole. I had a five-stroke lead and, for once, confidence was drowning out fear. A win! At last!

After a good drive, all that remained was an easy eight-iron over a stream, a couple putts, and laughter. When I dunked my first shot I was still three shots in the lead. No sweat. Then I plunked my second shot into the water, and the most dreaded word in golf exploded in my mind: *shank*, the near perfect swing that produces a ball that veers off to the right. Worse, shanks come in clusters. I was down simply to a one-shot lead.

As I began my back swing for the next shot, all the familiar sensations flooded me. There was the tightening of the throat, the proverbial apple to swallow. My muscles tightened, and I gripped the club like a lifeline, or, in that case, a death-line. Do you think I shanked away the remnant of my lead? That I snatched defeat from the jaws of victory? Even *I'd* never racked up a ten-stroke hole until it really mattered to me.

Terry looked on with glee and has never stopped gloating over my monumental choke. There was only a crowd of one, but it felt like the ninth inning at Yankee Stadium with the game on the line against the Red Sox.

The first step toward choking is the constant awareness that you can, and probably will. Just thinking of the *word* is a choke. Then there's the crowd. The outcome is inevitable. Choking is a nugget of disease buried in an otherwise happy life. It's the ball that breaks your heart. I feel it whenever I'm near the goddamn ball. At least by now I know what I can do about it. Nothing. And I know who's to blame. *Me.* The Choke Artist.

MULBERRY DOON

I SPEAK TO YOU TODAY AS DOON. Mulberry Doon. Please listen. The plant realm has always treated Mulberries and other Doons with detachment and disinterest: "Just another mulberry," they say. Humans see us only as generic fruits and trees. Sometimes even other trees seem to disrespect us. Perhaps its our own fault for being so close knit and clannish that the rest of creation has seemed insignificant to us. But I see, feel, and think, and I want to bring Mulberries into open view. We have rich lives and a world-view to share.

WHAT'S IN A NAME

If my name were Madogap Griunjiydd Maebov, I'd be recognized as a medieval Welsh prince. The King of Bhutan gets away with Signe Khesar Nameyel. Ten thousand Chinese are named Hop Li, and no one bats an eye. Every Arab is Mohamed el-Whatever His Hometown is. So I'm guessing that my name, Mulberry Doon, came from the Pict language—Doon the son of Mull back when the Romans ruled everything. The "berry" seals my fate as a humble fruit, and we are all Mull berries.

If your name happens to be Smith, your progenitors were probably blacksmiths. If you're a Black, it's the same. Gundersson is obvious, but after a few thousand Gundersson's sons, Nordic naming becomes trite. We have Mulligans, Mullherns, Mullers, and other Mulls to fill out our group. But when I think of the generations of Mulberries who have died unnoticed, unheard, and unmarked, I weep. I want to bring us recognition.

FAMILY FIRST

All Mulberries start with identical traumatic childhood experiences: extreme parental neglect. Parents drop us, often half ripe, and that's it. No Patty Cake or bedtime stories. We are white, red, or black mulberries. The first two are sour and tasteless, but black is sweet. Happily, I am a black mulberry. I still remember a young girl collecting a handful of unripe black mulberries and popping them into her mouth. The grimace on her face still haunts me when she recognized that they were tart and acid, like white mulberries. I've told myself, "It wasn't your fault she made a poor choice. Nature is to blame." Still, the look of surprised pain lingers. But it's that lack of parenting that leaves all Mulberries with a note of plangent emptiness. We don't even have sarcastic stories about Mom and Dad. We have what I call the Mulberry Hole in our identity.

What we lack in parenting skills, or even interest in parenting, we replace with strong sibling relationships. I keep up with all eighty siblings who shared our original teaspoon-sized fruit. We are our own most cherished possessions. Two thousand years ago, one Mulberry Doon brother was eaten by a dove and deposited on a cargo ship that landed in Italy. He reached Noto and went on to a verdant valley with steep stone cliffs housing ten thousand individual mausoleums carved into the vertical walls. Each tiny hewn cave housed a dead family member complete with a stone blocking the exit. This was the accepted Christian burial rite in pagan Rome and in 1 AD Judea. And yes, there were Mulberries observing the ancient entombment of Jesus. They saw it all. They know the whole story, but are sworn to secrecy. Sorry. *Now* are you interested in us?

Another of my contemporary sisters was eaten by a squirrel who found his way into the baggage hold of a flight to Kabul, Afghanistan. He froze, and my sisters starved, froze, and died fruitless. What an awful place: cold, barren, dry, rocky, primitive and punitive. Bad luck. Keep away from Kabul.

I have been luckier than most of my siblings. I was eaten by a chipmunk and deposited a mile from my birthplace in a comfortable New Jersey suburban neighborhood. Life is easy if a bit boring. I spread my boughs, relax, and have lots of bird visitors for diversion. Incidentally, mulberries don't soar, they spread, sometimes stopping as a mere bush. But we are sensitive and aware, and that has given us a window into man's various plights.

NOBODY KNOWS

the troubles I've seen. It was forgivable behavior for Homo Erectus and early Homo Sapiens to do anything to survive. They lived in cold, dark caves. Either you ate animals, or they ate you. Resources were scant, and if outside tribes invaded your territory, you killed them. If food was scarce, you ate them, too. Humans matched the brutality of their times. More remarkably, as need has shriveled, barbarism continues to flourish. Consider Darfur, the Holocaust, Stalinism, Hiroshima and Nagasaki, to name just a few. For humans, even science breeds slaughter. But if, at the fringes of my spreading boughs, I see a young chestnut sapling struggling, but full of promise, I spread my branches to rob it of sunshine. I send my roots to steal every drop of moisture. Saint Mulberry? Comfortable suburban street? It's still a jungle.

We start small, very small, pinhead small. The giants of the past, T-Rex and woolly mammoths, are now large historical footprints. Do you think elephants and rhinos will do better? We plants were here first and will be here last. You need us. We don't need you. It's safer to be small and tough, preferably with a hard seed coat. We need less food and water to make it as Hard Times Charlies. Our mulberry seeds will sprout millennia from now, when testosterone, the elixir of death, is long forgotten. We plants and trees know the ropes. We *are* the ropes.

We mulberries have seen it all. Man, beast, and plant are all predators, and the parents of future predators. Each of us wants my food and water, my sunshine, and my space. Long live my DNA. And if you're thinking of making a pie, leave us alone and pick on blueberries. They're stupid. I know. Trust me.

Poems

MANY OF THE FOLLOWING POEMS *were written between* 3:00 AM *and* 6:00 AM, *quiet, alone, prime poetry time. Hence, they almost qualify as dreams. Some have annotations; some do not. Most poets disparage editorials and explanations, but they then expostulate when reading their poetry. I do it in the book for the same reason. I hope that it helps the reader.*

"Hide and Seek" and "Spring Training" call forth fond childhood sounds and memories. The following melange of poems touches on art, parody, and cosmology (that again). It is satirical in tone and largely upbeat.

The next four poems are a family section introducing three new poets. Sara Milano and Evelyn Burgess are granddaughters, and Sean is our youngest son. Some poetry gene seems to be running around in our family, and it should be nurtured. Pat's poem completes the family poetry.

"Whiteness: For Ernie" ushers in a change of tone. The poems are deeper, sadder, and, I think better. Love, loss, and transition speak forcefully to all of us. "Living well is letting go" is one of several responses to these feelings.

HIDE AND SEEK

One Mississippi, two Mississippi,
three Mississippi, four. . . .

Dare I peek between my fingers?
Do the others do it?
Is it fair or is it cheating?
Where'd I hide if I wasn't It?
Can I speed the Mississippis?
Nine Mississippi, ten Mississippi. . . .

Free to run, free to hide, free to seek:
Ready or not, here I come.

SPRING TRAINING

Fetch the fielder's glove
from the downstairs closet,
kindling dreams of backhand stops
and making the pivot: 6-4-3.

Massage the hardened leather
with warm Neet's Foot Oil.
(What's a Neet, and how did it
sacrifice its foot for my glove?)

Next wrap the glove
around a ball and lace
them tightly. Slip the pair beneath
your mattress, where your body shapes the pocket.

The Princess and the Pea,
the dreamer and his glove,
the sleeper and his dreamcatcher,
make spring training take wing.

Play ball!

WE MAY NOT BE ALONE

Scientists currently estimate that the universe
contains forty billion planets "in the Goldilocks Zone,"
i.e., neither too hot nor too cold to support life.

Hey there, you with the stars in your eyes,*
hubris just made a fool of you,
promised that God made this for you
and made you his grandiose prize.

If 4.5 billion earths spin in the Milky Way,
do twenty-three angels dance on the head of a pin?
Are there a billion more galaxies
bathed in an ether of when?

After three thousand years of searching the skies,
Ptolemy and Aristotle thought they had it right.
Earth is the center, circled by the sun,
and mankind rules all within sight.

Then Copernicus and Galileo designed
a universe ruled by just math,

where earth spins round the sun, the king,
and others may mimic our path.

I'd like to meet the skinny green ones
with bulging eyes and three fingers.
I wonder if they speak English
or merely go, *Beep, beep, beep*.

Will they invade us, bugger us,
or simply steal all of our females?
Then we'll all be popeyed and pea green
some day, if you know what I mean.

Are they in heaven reveling in
country, Bach, or Roxy Music?
Republicans, Democrats, or gasp,
socialists cohabiting our galaxy.

If, somewhere, they look exactly like us
and fight, and pray, and vow
they are chosen ones,
they're wrong. It's us. I know.

And if this infinity of space
holds an infinity of creatures

exactly like us, someday we'll meet
and share our universality, and have

one helluva party.

*"Hey There," song from *Pajama Game*,
created by Adler and Ross, 1954.

BUZZED

A certain feeling comes
after a martini,
some sauvignon blanc,
two glasses of zin,
and a scotch or brandy or two.

Ritual's important here.
Booze is the poetry that
fuses with the piano, that
dances quick and slow,
refreshing all the old stories.
battling the sodden thrust of sleep.

Buzz. . .zzz

John Updike is a renowned poet with a large body of work. Dave Etter, on the other hand, is a regional poet who sings, with lots of local color, of rural and small town Ohio. The poem, another send up, uses typical Etter language. "When You Are Grey" spoofs Yeats's poem of the same name. His poem is deep and mysterious. Google it.

UPDIKE, DOWNSTREAM

By now the readers know my name—
my books, my honors, and the fuss
that swirled around my head, as fame
became a pain in my *tochis*.

In twenty-odd books
I probed the odd habits
of middle-class kooks,
the Smiths and the Rabbits.

For sodomite, oralist,
missionary, doggie lover,
I gave sex the twist
suburban squares love to savor.

Of Zeus, Clytemnestra,
I hunger to speak.
You see, I've confessed a
love for old Greek.

But my heart lay in rhyme,
Angels' heavenly bread,
where I now spend my time—
since I'm thoroughly dead.

HOMARD TO DAVE ETTER

The majority of America, coast to coast,
should be southern Illinois.
But not Chicago, where they butcher
cows instead of raising them.
In Smiley's dingy Golden Bar,
the plumber, Old Man Joe,
allowed that maple leaves
from up north had a nice crunch
but didn't soak up rainwater
like those in Effingham or
Ratchahatchee or Manachuk.
Way down south, both the names of their
Indians and their food sound strange to us,
even though they use a lot of corn.
As I laid some river thorn rose
hickeys on Doreen's double D's,
I felt the railroad, Wabash or Soo Line,
running through this verse like
liquid sheep dip through Miles Davis's horn.
It's time to pick your country cornflowers
before they turn a dusty Sandberg brown.

WHEN YOU ARE OLD AND GREY*

When you are old and grey,
having stopped coloring your hair,
take down this poem and
remember that at least he tried
to find your pilgrim soul,
even if he ended up odd and cranky,
as all old men do. Even Yeats.

*"When You Are Old & Grey," *William Butler Yeats*

NATURE

Frankly I don't give a damn
about nature. Never did.
Daffodils, with two F's, and
jonquils, with a J and a Q,
are clever words worthy of
more extensive use than for
blooms that are donne in weeks.

Weather's often just the rod
of nature's punishment.
Redwoods soar and
willows weep. Marvelous,
but can they really heal or
hurt you? How then do
they earn our worship?

I'd give nature a second look
if there were no books around,
or games, sports, TV, or
music. Give me just one
person with wit or a good story,

and you can have the sunsets.
They're all pretty much the same.

INNERVISION

When ego looked down on the soul,
it saw something resembling a hole.

There is little to learn from the rock,
ten thousand pebbles fused into one.
No knowledge can see through its block.

Bearers of opacity, these sullen planes,
sexless nuns decrying passion,
allow no insight, no love or gains.

When libido looked up at the soul,
it winked at whatever looked holy.

POETRY

Poetry is
the alchemy
of words.

THE ROSE

I bought one red rose,
seeking to explore beauty.
Still tightly bound with
symmetrical leaves, it held
the heart of symphonic desire.

For a week I watched the
fist relax and a shower of
red, yellow, blue, and green
emerge, then turn brown.
Next, to my surprise,
a phalanx of aphids left
the fading bloom. Grandeur
had begun its decline and
I, the poet, would be able to
study death, and beauty turned rot.

Gently the bloom nodded,
Rose, aphid, and death
becoming one. The rose's
unfruited head, shorn,

bowed in resignation.
The cycle complete, the stalk,
no longer the green fuse of life,
stood bare save a procession of
thorns. Its final comment
on beauty now awaited the unwary. . . .

THE ROSE 2

Pride, weasel, rainbow.
Start the oil-slicked motor,
run it backwards
until aphid and rose
are rose-aphid,
wing and petal and all.

Writing about medicine and psychiatry has come to me surprisingly late. The next four poems are those about a patient (me) and a psychotherapist.

WAITING FOR SURGERY

Something there is that doesn't
love a knife. It's the waiting,
the waiting alone for the body
to be opened like a book
to read its entrails.

Four AM. The silken black sky
and the calm of the surgery floor
anesthetize my anxiety.
"Comforting night and stars,
could you linger three more hours?"

Five AM. The sun is ascendant and
the bustle of the floor begins.
Bloods are drawn, "vitals" taken
and sleep vanishes hours before
the gurney arrives.

"Be patient. You're first
on the list." Elsewhere,
in a simple, undecorated room,
loved ones wait to hear
the surgeon say, "Everything went well."

Probably.

THUNDER FOR THE DEAF, DIAMONDS FOR THE BLIND

(On phobia and depression)

My patient plied a simple trade,
washing windows. Not for
stores or homes, for skyscrapers
thirty, forty, fifty stories high.
Thought nothing of it.
Everyday was music.

The day that he retired,
the thunder went completely still,
and he never left his house alone.
The earth seemed too laced
with danger. Fear cast a pall
of silence over his courage.

Another patient, gifted
with money, marriage,
robust children, and his own
successful business, saw his
starlit path vanish when

depression and despair came.

There was no blessing in his
hopelessness and fear.
Blackness hid the truth and the future.
In his solitude, no light or joy
entered or escaped him.

So life is as we feel it,
never what it is.
We live subjectively,
prisoners of hidden
mechanisms, born
upon our inner winds.

DEMENTIA

Now that
the past has eaten the future and
the hours are measured in echoes and

now that
the boat without a rudder drifts and
the river has no banks and

now that
the days are dreamless sleep and
the nights are seamless hell and

now that
the faces have become blind and
the words have become mute and

now that
the tumbling ideas have stilled and
the symbols lost their substance and

now that

our love has lost its way and
left me empty and alone and

now. . .that. . . .

NOTHING HAS
NO CONSEQUENCES

For those of my patients
not yet broken in their
body, who chose
hopelessness over love
and took an early end—
you left us with the burden of why.

Anger is a well-honed razor
that slices off the lesions
of caring and guilt, leaving no
memory, no connection to you.
My friends, be forewarned!
Nothing has no consequences.

Univocal lipograms are a rarefied poetic pleasure. Restricting the poem to one vowel forces more fluid conjunctions of words. Unusual combinations emerge. "OH" is a pure lipogram, using the letter "o". It is dominated by sound and begs to be spoken. "no i" highlights the letter "i". Later on, "Palynology" dances with "o". Both of the latter are lipogramish.

OH

Too soon noon's groom
grows old, not bold.
So look to only joy.
Don't mock fools
who don doom's togs.

Gloom or fog or frown
show chords of dolor.
Sow blossoms, not roots,
or toys for sooty rooms
or soft loops of cozy down.

Don't opt for goofy
looks, odd norms
for old, worn toms

who took hog loot
for vows of lofty concord.

Zoom to topmost honors.

no i

There is no "i" in team
or poetry or even sex.
Ego, that ancient Roman I,
incites the quarterback,
the versifier, and the
multitudes pursuing passion.

It is all about applause
and recognition: a
thundering stadium, a
knot of poetry lovers, or,
best of all, a partner
who says, "You're the greatest.".

If you have to have an "i,"
try jai-alai, haiku, or
i-sex, masturbation.
The rewards are tinier,
but the risks are miniscule,

your highness.

The next two poems are about visual artists. Wolfgang Laib, a German minimalist and spiritualist, has many signature works of Milkstones and beeswax sculptures. "Pollen From Hazelnut," the exhibit that inspired this poem, was a bed of pollen spread on the floor of the atrium of the New York City Museum Of Modern Art in 2013. Its pure yellow was unmatched in intensity and shouted "nature." Google him.

PALYNOLOGY*

Golden sower,
pollen of the laurel,
you will never grow into
a crown of joy or hope.
      How sad.

Wolfgang Laib has
stolen you, housed you at
the MOMA, and sifted you into
a graceful lake of sunshine.
      How beautiful.

Elsewhere he makes

magic mounds, pollen
volcanoes, nature's wit
crouching in a corner.
　　　How mysterious.

Alder, pine,
dandelion, sorrel,
buttercup, hazelnut:
These are the roots of beauty.
　　　How fundamental.

Let the eye look
to the soul, but
never ask the question:
"Does it hurt the flowers?"
　　　Everything matters.

Palynology: The study of pollen

Ad Reinhardt is a singular minimalist. The tonalities of his paintings are as subtle as the structure is severe. It takes some time to grasp what's laid out on a nine-block tic-tac-toe grid. Look at the paintings from the side, then head-on. Unfortunately, Reinhardt doesn't reproduce well.

AD REINHARDT

never was an easy painter.
On first examination, head-on,
he shows us nothing
but black sameness.
Seen from the side,
the red, green, blue—
always just those three—
barely find expression
through panes of matte black paint.

Is this a metaphor of the body,
messages emerging from the heart,
from muscles and the gut: red, blue, green?
Do perceptions cloaked from casual scrutiny
struggle for recognition from

A superstition

If you want to be perfect
Change your definition

—*Sara Milano*

DOWN-TO-EARTH

Rooted plants
cross the borders of the core
through the molten lava,
moments of sacrifice
everything so remote
in an unusual tempo
with instances of overwhelming exhaustion;
the goal was unclear
and the intentions were skewed
but I was devoted
and it was beyond my control;
then,
abruptly
I felt growth.

—*Evelyn Burgess*

ILLUMINATES

Great Sleep,
What more doth speak
Where fools suppose
Their souls to keep:
A ransom stacked
For those who weep.

A darkness visible on the face
Of the deep Illuminates
The quantum leap.
Pray don't tell a step that creaks;
Be all there is for priests to seek.

—*Sean Milano*

i carry your heart

(with apologies to e.e. cummings)

i carry your heart
with its bypass and grafts,
"cabbage" they call it,
now with a stent,
on plavix,
i carry your clotting times and meds,
your medtronic number
and medicare card.

i carry them
as you fight on for life,
for longevity,
for more time together,
i carry your heart with all its protrusions
and wires,
because you gave it to me.

—*Patricia Milano*

WHITENESS: FOR ERNIE

It's not as if the sun
won't shine again
and bring new blossoms
every April,
nor will the ball refuse
to fly off eighteen tees,
straight and long,
golf on July the Fourth.

But just this morning,
Utica is sheathed
in newborn white,
the Chinese dress of mourning.
January grace descends
from my clouds of grief, announcing
that this sheen of flawless white
will forever separate us.

Hold close the daily dance
of past, our lasting recollections.
They bind us, though

no further hands will
deepen our connection.
So the lightness, the whiteness,
the years of loving laughter,
will keep you in my heart forever.
Forever.

GRATITUDE

It's been a giddy life,
afloat on deepest joy
and laughter, and of love.

You know who you are:
eight and seven and more
to come, rewards beyond

my wildest expectations,
core of my life
for five or seven decades.

You know who you are
and what you've meant.
To you and to the shining rings

of friends and family
who brought me to this blessed
life, be deeply honored and thanked.

HANDS

Hello, hands, the mangled
servants of my lifetime.
Pain sustains awareness.
It's acceptable.
What's not is clumsiness:
aging, twitching vicars
fumbling with a tiny collar button.

At ten years of age, facile minions
marched to the drill of Miss Whelan,
the spinster princess of sonatinas,
playing Chopin and Hanon exercises.
The trill and the scale in triads asked
my hands for an elusive skill
they never quite possessed.

Thickened hands grip and re-grip
the seven iron, hoping to overcome
past futility. Strong right, weak right,
the left hand struggles to accommodate
the growing estrangement

of eye, brain, and hand.
Experiment is futile.

Sweet irony: The hands of love
grow ever stronger, smoother,
and more gentle.
They no longer fumble or doubt when
these hands touch your face,
your hair, your body. These hands
grow younger every year.

COLLATERAL DAMAGE

Consider light rain
glazing the red wheelbarrow.*
It flashes, then returns to cloud.
But a fraction,
molecule by molecule,
sifts to deeper layers
of shale and rock
to be our hidden reservoirs.

Water drifting downward,
Nature's unfelt breathing,
adds nuance to materiality.
Inner layers accept, soften, and
cherish the rewards of seepage.
It's the hidden part that thrills,
that creates the aquifer.

Romantic love glistens, too.
Beauty and a smile strike the flame.
Whoever had been dry and self-absorbed
now flows and rejoices, bringing too

the sadness of losing love and leaving beloved.
New joy, new meaning, seep into our core,
bringing the promise of future loss.

Call it collateral damage.

*"*The Red Wheelbarrow,*" William Carlos Williams

LONGHAND

The scrawl of girls, now ladies
still grieving for the boys
who went to Nam
and never came back.
The penmanship of voices past,
of Kukla, Fran and Ollie,
of Peter, Paul and Mary,
the tracings of my longhand youth.
Your left hand in my right,
I on the sidewalk fringe
poised to repel marauders,
a longhand custom of the past.

Kiss the paper, timepebbles, childskips,
the script of the past is in the now.

A PERSONAL POEM

The poker players
art lovers
sports fans
golfers
tennis players

The doctors
wine makers
musicians
chess players and
poetry fanatics
visit me often these nights.

Why do they crowd my sleep
when the present and the future
feel so deep and good?
Why these dreams, so many, and so often?
Is it nostalgia rich with gratitude,
or are they my brothers
of the long sleep?

HAIKU

Crystal drops on fallen leaves,
Wild geese flying south. . .
Living well is letting go.

A LIFE OF MOURNING

A life of mourning dawned
for me in childhood. After
losing a parent, my father,
my love of the piano also
disappeared, like salt in water.
Practicing Hanon and Czerny
without him was futile.

The music of my grief
transposed into one long soft note,
sostenendo, almost imperceptible
amid the clatter of a
happy life of comfort and success.
It played modestly, like the
viola in the "Andante Cantabile"
in Tchaikovsky's String Quartet in D.
It clung to love's remembrance,
a stately duet with the echo of loss.

Slowly, *largetto, poco a poco,*
the pedal point, the drone

of separation, has moved
from the past into the present.
My new mourning, awareness of
coming loss, is for you and
for me. For what we are together
and what we have created.

Ritardando, slow it down,
let the rondo play and play.
Life without your laughter,
music in a somber key, soon
enough will play its final chord.
Mourning the present reveres
the joy that lives today. Our
sadness and joy both sing of now.
A life of mourning is a life of love.